The Day Whishka Lost His Purr

Annabelle Christina

Balboa Press books may be ordered through booksellers or by contacting:

Balboa Press
A Division of Hay House
1663 Liberty Drive
Bloomington, IN 47403
www.balboapress.com.au
1 (877) 407-4847

This is a work of fiction. All of the characters, names, incidents, organizations, and dialogue in this novel are either the products of the author's imagination or are used fictitiously.

ISBN: 978-1-5043-1412-1 (sc)
ISBN: 978-1-5043-1413-8 (e)

Print information available on the last page.

Balboa Press rev. date: 12/07/2018

BALBOA
PRESS
A DIVISION OF HAY HOUSE

It was a still, starry, springtime night over the city. The city mirrored the sky with all its bright lights. Number 5 Glade Street was quiet with sleep. Underneath the staircase was a large basket lined with a deep soft cushion in which Nikiesha, a chocolate-tipped, big-eared, pointy-faced Burmese pussycat, slept, snuggled up with her five kittens: Muffles, Scruffles, Twinkle, Puffin and Whishka; all purring in their sleep.

Suddenly, there was a flash of light through the house. It *flitted* over five year old Rosy as she stirred in her bed. It *zoomed* through the study where Computer was softly whirring. It *swooshed* past ancient Grandfather Clock as he sounded 4 am in the hallway. It buzzed quietly around the basket of kittens. It zipped through the kitchen as Fridge gave a hefty sigh.

It darted swiftly over Sandy, the plump golden retriever, snuffling in his sleep near the back door before it dashed away through the open window into the garden. There was a hushed rustle of leaves in the corner of the garden and then all was quiet and still again.

Gradually the sky turned from dark blue, to lilac, to pale blue with streaks of pink as dawn broke and the household began to wake.

In the basket under the staircase Whishka stirred and snuggled up closer against Nikeisha and all his brothers and sisters. Nikeisha and all Whishka's brothers and sisters purred but something was wrong. Whishka opened his big sleepy eyes and a frown creased his little furry brow. He snuggled again, even closer amongst his family. Everybody was purring. Everyone, that is, except for Whishka. An even bigger frown creased his little furry brow.

When it was time for breakfast Rosy poured out fresh cream for all the kittens in the kitchen. They lapped it up with fast pink tongues, purring as they drank. All of them, that is, except for Whiska who sat back and looked around at his brothers and sisters. He looked very worried.

In the sitting room, after breakfast, Whishka sat there silent and miserable. Rosy came over to him and picked him up for a cuddle. He looked silently up at her. Still nothing was happening.

"What's wrong Whishka?" Rosy asked.

"I don't know", Whishka sobbed, "When I woke up this morning my purr had gone."

"Oh my goodness", Rosy exclaimed, "You can't be a happy kitten until you've found your purr! Someone must know what has happened to it. Ask everybody. I'm sure someone will be able to help you find it."

Whishka's brothers and sisters come tumbling into the sitting room to play.

"Muffles, Scruffles, Twinkle and Puffin" Whishka said. All his siblings paused mid-play to look questioningly at him. "I seem to have lost my purr. Do any of you know what has happened to it?"

Muffles, Scruffles, Twinkle and Puffin all started laughing hysterically. They guffawed, hooted, squealed, rolled and tumbled around the floor - they were laughing so hard.

Muffles cried, "Lost your purr? What do you mean you lost your purr? How can you possibly lose your purr?" before he tumbled down onto the carpet laughing again.

Just then, Nikeisha strolled in.

"What's wrong Whishka?" she asked.

Whishka sighed, "I seem to have lost my purr. I can't find it anywhere."

Nikeisha comforted him, "Now, now Sweetkins, I'm sure if you search very carefully you'll find your purr again. It must be somewhere."

"I know", Whiska sighed again, "I'll keep looking", and he trudged sadly out of the room.

In the kitchen, Whishka sat and looked up enquiringly at Fridge. Fridge was grumpy as usual.

"You 'right there? What's the matter then? You're not hungry again are you? As if you little monsters didn't store enough fat under your fur…" Fridge grumbled.

Whishka explained, "Please Sir, it's just that…well…I seem to have lost my purr."

"Well not everything's about purring my boy is it? We all have our troubles boy. See this seal here…" Fridge flung open his door and a portion of the seal around his door crackled and bent. He flung the door shut again.

Whishka sighed and interrupted, "Well thank you anyway Sir…" and he left to continue his search.

Whishka paused in front of old Grandfather Clock. "Yeeeeeeeeeeeeeuuuuuuuuuuuuus," he said peering down at little Whishka.

"Excuse me for disturbing you Sir", apologised Whishka, "but it's really very important."

"What can be so important that you find it necessary to disturb me?" Groaned the giant clock.

"It's my purr, Sir", Whishka pleaded, "It appears to have gone missing and I was hoping…"

"I have stood here in this hallway for 100 years, 216 days, 9 hours, 58 minutes and… 47 seconds," Grandfather Clock growled, "Do you think I would care if I saw a purr wandering by? So run along now and leave me be."

In the study, Whishka scrambled up onto the desk and peered at Computer. He swiftly tossed Computer's mouse from side to side with his paws before stepping across the keyboard. The screen lit up with a picture of a beautiful snow encrusted mountain range with peaceful lake-filled valleys.

"You are troubled my son", Computer observed.

"Yes, Sir", replied Whishka.

"I feel you have lost something", Computer continued.

"Yes indeed, Sir!" Whishka nodded hopefully.

"It is something important to how you express yourself."

"Yes, Sir! My purr!" cried Whishka.

Computer paused, "I sensed a disturbance…."

"Really Sir?" cried Whishka.

Computer continued, "At about 4 o'clock this morning…there was…er"

"Yes, Sir". implored Whishka.

But before Computer could continue he made a sudden loud whirring, humming, grunting noise and his screen went still and black.

Whishka sighed, jumped down from the desk and plodded gloomily out of the study.

Sandy was snuffling in the midst of his mid-morning snooze. He half opened one eye and glared suspiciously at Whishka approaching.

Whishka looked at him wide-eyed, "Excuse me Sir, it's my purr. I seem to have lost it and I was wondering if you might have some idea of what may have happened to it since you're in charge of security. Computer suggested that something may have happened at around 4 am this morning."

Sandy thought for a moment. "Hmm…yes…last night, I thought I saw the Wish Fairy sneaking out through that window and her briefcase seemed heavier than usual. You should ask her what happened to your purr."

"The Wish Fairy?" exclaimed Whiska, "Do you know where I might find her, Sir?"

"Hmm", said Sandy, "Sometimes she naps under the purple flowering bush in the garden. She might still be there but you'll have to wait until she wakes up at dusk."

"Thank you so much Sir!" exclaimed Whishka eagerly and he struggled his way out of the cat-flap and trotted out into the garden.

Sure enough, under a shelter of little purple flowers Whishka found the Wish Fairy sleeping, pillowed by her diamond-speckled briefcase and covered in a blanket of leaves. He curled up patiently nearby to wait for dusk.

Slowly, as the afternoon wore on, the sky changed from cloudy blue to lilac with orange streaks in the West.

There was a sudden rustle of leaves and Whishka sprung up excitedly. The Wish Fairy stumbled dozily out from under the bush. She was not much taller than Whishka, had very tall scruffy hair set with a sparkly crown and wore a short suit which kept changing colours as she moved and had specially designed holes in the back for her long, pointy, diamond-speckled wings. She gave a very large, very sleepy yawn looking dozily at Whishka before her eyes suddenly widened and she leapt upwards towards the sky holding her briefcase close.

"But, but, wait, wait Ma'am! I just need to ask you something…It's very important", Whishka cried, "I just want to ask you whether…" yelled Whishka and he jumped and leapt up as high as he possibly could and the edge of one of his claws caught the side of the Wish Fairy's briefcase.

As Whishka fell back to earth pulling down the Wish Fairy's briefcase, it sprung open and out of it floated down to the ground a soft, see-through, purring, glowing, golden globe.

"…My purr!" shrieked Whishka and he quickly jumped onto the glowing, golden globe and rolled on it back and forth, back and forth until it was safely back inside of him and he was purring proudly and loudly.

The Wish Fairy hovered there for a moment and then slowly flapped her way down to earth, flush-faced with embarrassment.

"Why Ma'am? Why?" Whishka glared at her.

The Wish Fairy lowered her head.

"Listen kid, have you any idea how many wishes I receive every single day of the year. I mean we're talking billions of needy children and billions more of spoilt little brats who think they're needy - get the picture? How can the Wish Fairy satisfy everyone if she drops dead of over-work – huh? So I need a little shortcut here and there."

"But what has this got to do with my…" began Whishka.

"You know a little bit of "purr-power" goes a long way, do you understand? It saves me time and energy and I get back my social life. Did you know that I haven't been out on a date for a hundred years?"

Whishka nodded slowly and sadly, "I understand Ma'am but…you know, all you had to do was ask."

The Wish Fairy blushed.

"I'm sorry kid." She patted him on the head. "Do you really mean that? That all I have to do is ask? Can you fly? Do you think we might discuss some kind of arrangement? I really could do with a paw, so-to-speak…" The Wish Fairy ruffled the fur behind Whishka's ears and started telling him about all the adventures they could have together helping children with the power of Whishka's special little purr.

THE END

Printed in the United States
By Bookmasters